ONE HUG

Written by **Katrina Moore**   Illustrated by **Julia Woolf**

KATHERINE TEGEN BOOKS
An Imprint of HarperCollins Publishers

Hugs & Love,
K.Moore

One Hug

ISBN 978-0-06-284954-0

The artist used ArtPrint printers ink by Seawhite of Brighton
and Photoshop to create the digital illustrations for this book.
Typography by Rachel Zegar
19   20   21   22   23   SCP   10   9   8   7   6   5   4   3   2   1
❖
First Edition

To Penelope, Benjamin, and Keith,
who give the best snuggles
—K.M.

For Kate and all her animals
—J.W.

One hug.

Two hugs.

Sometimes three.

Hugging makes us family.

Some hugs nuzzle nose to nose.

Some hugs *lick* and tickle toes!

Chasing, racing, to and fro,
sometimes hugs are *on the go*!

Open arms that swoop around,
some hugs *whoosh* you off the ground.

Some hugs wait for years and years.

Some hugs cradle falling tears.

Some hugs spin you super fast.

Other hugs were made to last.

One might need a hug right now.

Could you help to show them how?

Lean in close and nestle in?

Wow! You made a frown a grin.

Warm and sweet like Grandma's tea, hugging makes us family.

Catching, cupping,
not too tight,

some hugs twinkle in the night.

Grabbing bundles, one,

two,

three,

one hug turns a "me" to "we."

Lullabies and starlit skies,
one big snuggle, sleeeepy eyes.

Curled up. Cuddly. Cozily.
How do YOU hug family?